GROUNDHOG DAY

PHIL

by Betsy Lewin

Hello Reader! — Level 1

SCHOLASTIC INC.

New York Toronto London Auckland Sydney
Mexico City New Delhi Hong Kong

Everyone is waiting for Phil, the groundhog, to wake up and come out of his burrow.

If it's cloudy, Phil won't see his shadow, and he will stay outside. That means spring will come soon.

If it's sunny, Phil will see his shadow.
He will go back inside his burrow
and there will be six more weeks
of winter.

But Phil is still asleep
in his dark, warm bed.

Suddenly, Phil is lifted up,
high in the air.

Everyone cheers!

Then, Phil is on
the cold ground.
He takes a few steps
and looks around.

No shadow.

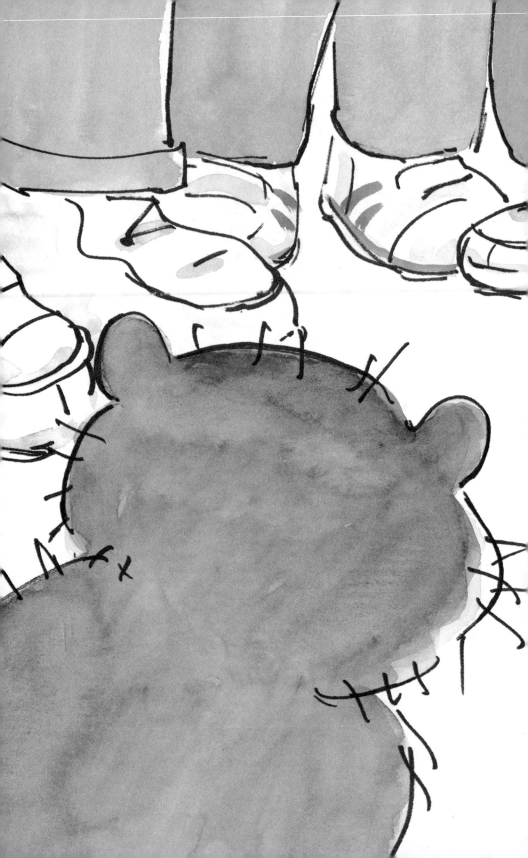

He sees lots and lots
of feet,
but no shadow.

He looks up and sees
a cold, gray sky,
but no shadow.

The crowd shouts, "**HOORAY!**

Phil does not see his shadow.
Spring is on the way!"

Phil hears a big "**CLICK!**"
A light flashes.
The light makes a shadow!

"EEK!" squeaks Phil.
He dives back into his burrow.

All these years, people thought
it was the weather.
Now we know the truth.
Phil is afraid of his own shadow!